A Note to Parents

For many children, learning math is difficult and "I hate math!" is their first response — to which many parents silently add "Me, too!" Children often see adults comfortably reading and writing, but they rarely have such models for mathematics. And math fear can be catching!

The easy-to-read stories in this **Hello Math** series were written to give children a positive introduction to mathematics and parents a pleasurable re-acquaintance with a subject that is important to everyone's life. **Hello Math** stories make mathematical ideas accessible, interesting, and fun for children. The activities and suggestions at the end of each book provide parents with a hands-on approach to help children develop mathematical interest and confidence.

Enjoy the mathematics!
• Give your child a chance to retell the story. The more familiar children are with the story, the more they will understand its mathematical concepts.
• Use the colorful illustrations to help children "hear and see" the math at work in the story.
• Treat the math activities as games to be played for fun. Follow your child's lead. Spend time on those activities that engage your child's interest and curiosity.
• Activities, especially ones using physical materials, help make abstract mathematical ideas concrete.

Learning is a messy process and learning about math calls for children to become immersed in lively experiences that help them make sense of mathematical concepts and symbols.

Although learning about numbers is basic to math, other ideas, such as identifying shapes and patterns, measuring, collecting and interpreting data, reasoning logically, and thinking about chance are also important. By reading these stories and having fun with the activities, you will help your child enthusiastically say **"Hello, Math,"** instead of "I hate math."

—Marilyn Burns
National Mathematics Educator
Author of *The I Hate Mathematics! Book*

To Ryan
— Aunt Gracie

To Paul, with love
—M.H.

Copyright © 1998 by Scholastic Inc.
The activities on pages 26-32 copyright © 1998 by Marilyn Burns.
All rights reserved. Published by Scholastic Inc.
HELLO MATH READER and CARTWHEEL BOOKS and associated logos are trademarks and/or registered trademarks of Scholastic Inc.

Library of Congress Cataloging-in-Publication Data
Maccarone, Grace.
    Monster math picnic/by Grace Maccarone; math activities by Marilyn Burns; illustrated by Marge Hartelius.
        p.   cm. — (Hello math reader. Level 1)
    Summary: The number of monsters engaged in various activities at a picnic always adds up to ten. Includes related activities.
    ISBN 0-590-37127-4
    [1. Monsters—Fiction.   2. Counting.   3. Stories in rhyme.]
    I. Burns, Marilyn.   II. Hartelius, Margaret A., ill.   III. Title.
    IV. Series.
PZ8.3.M127Mp   1998
[E]—dc21   97-12854
                                                                              CIP
                                                                              AC

10 9 8 7 6 5 4 3 2 1   8 9/9 0/0 01 02

Printed in the U.S.A.   24
First printing, March 1998

Monster
Math

Picnic

by Grace Maccarone
Illustrated by Marge Hartelius
Math Activities by Marilyn Burns

Hello Math Reader — Level 1

SCHOLASTIC INC.
Cartwheel ·B·O·O·K·S·®

New York Toronto London Auckland Sydney

Are the monsters ready to go?

Ten say yes. Zero say no.

Nine monsters come by air.

One monster comes by land.

Eight monsters play in mud.

Two monsters play in sand.

Seven chase squirrels.

Three chase bears.

Six sit on benches.

Four sit on chairs.

Five monsters eat some bread.

Five monsters eat some cheese.

Four monsters run from flies.

Six monsters run from bees.

Three swim.

Seven just float.

Two surf.

Eight sail a boat.

One monster wants to rest.

Nine monsters want to play.

Ten monsters go to sleep

and dream about their happy day.

• ABOUT THE ACTIVITIES •

Ten is a particularly important number in our number system, and young children have many opportunities to become familiar with it. They count ten fingers and ten toes. They learn that it takes ten pennies to make a dime and ten dimes to make a dollar. And they find out later that writing numbers depends on the ones' place, the tens' place, the hundreds' place, and so on.

While *Monster Math Picnic* can be enjoyed by children as a counting book, it also provides the additional benefit of encouraging children to think about the different combinations of addends that make ten. The story shows the combinations of ten in a logical sequence with the numbers in the combinations changing by one each time—10 + 0, 9 + 1, 8 + 2, and so on. Presenting the combinations in a pattern helps children see orderliness in mathematics.

The activities that follow suggest ways for children to think about how the number ten can be taken apart and put together in different ways. While the focus is on the number ten, the activities also work well with smaller numbers. Playing the games with smaller numbers can help your child build the confidence needed to understand larger quantities. Be open to your child's interests, and have fun with math!

—Marilyn Burns

You'll find tips and suggestions
for guiding the activities whenever
you see a box like this!

Retelling the Story

There are ten monsters in the story, so you need to have ten counters. You can use pennies, buttons, or beans. Count them out loud to be sure you have exactly ten. You also need two pieces of paper, each large enough to hold all ten counters.

The book starts, "Are the monsters ready to go? Ten say yes. Zero say no." Put all of the counters on one piece of paper. You should have ten counters on one paper and zero counters on the other paper.

Next the book says, "Nine monsters come by air. One monster comes by land." Now put nine counters on one piece of paper. Be sure there is one counter on the other paper.

Read the rest of the book and move the counters to show what happens on each page.

Monster Riddles

Here are riddles about other things the ten monsters could do at a picnic. Use ten counters to help you answer these riddles.

Seven monsters played tag.
How many monsters played catch?

Four monsters ate apples.
How many monsters ate pears?

Two monsters took naps.
How many monsters played hide-and-seek?

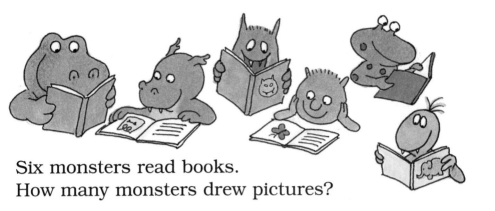

Six monsters read books.
How many monsters drew pictures?

Five monsters chased a squirrel.
How many monsters chased birds?

One monster built in the sand.
How many monsters went swimming?

Eight monsters looked for pebbles.
How many monsters looked for flowers?

Nine monsters wanted to play.
How many monsters wanted to clean up?

Ten monsters ate dessert.
How many monsters didn't eat?

Number Sentences

Number sentences can tell about the math happening in the story. For example, when eight monsters play in mud and two monsters play in sand, you can write 8 + 2 = 10. The number sentence says that eight monsters plus two monsters equal ten monsters.

You can show 8 + 2 like this:

You can write number sentences about 10 to tell about every page in the book.

10 + 0 = 10	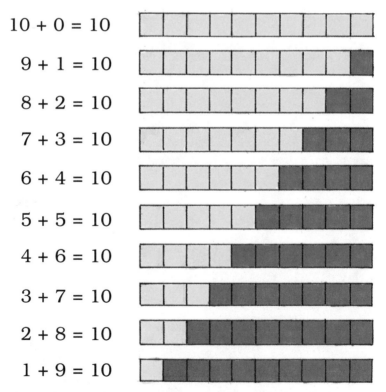
9 + 1 = 10	
8 + 2 = 10	
7 + 3 = 10	
6 + 4 = 10	
5 + 5 = 10	
4 + 6 = 10	
3 + 7 = 10	
2 + 8 = 10	
1 + 9 = 10	

Check in the story and match each number sentence with what the monsters did.

How Many Are Hiding?

This is a game for two people. You need ten counters.

Hide some of the counters in one hand and the rest of the counters in the other hand.

Your partner taps one of your hands. Open it and both of you count the counters.

Your partner tells how many counters are hiding in your other hand.

Open your other hand and count to check.

Take turns hiding the counters.

Because it's hard to visualize ten objects, it can be difficult for some children to know how many objects are left after some are hidden. If this game seems too hard for your child, practice first with smaller numbers of objects. Start with five objects and move up to six or seven as your child becomes comfortable.

Take Ten!

Put 15 or 20 dried beans, buttons, or other small things into a bowl. Then reach into the bowl and take some. Count. Did you take more than ten, fewer than ten, or exactly ten? Try again, taking things and counting them.